snow music

BY Lynne Rae Perkins

Greenwillow Books
An Imprint of HarperCollins*Publishers*

Everyone whisper:

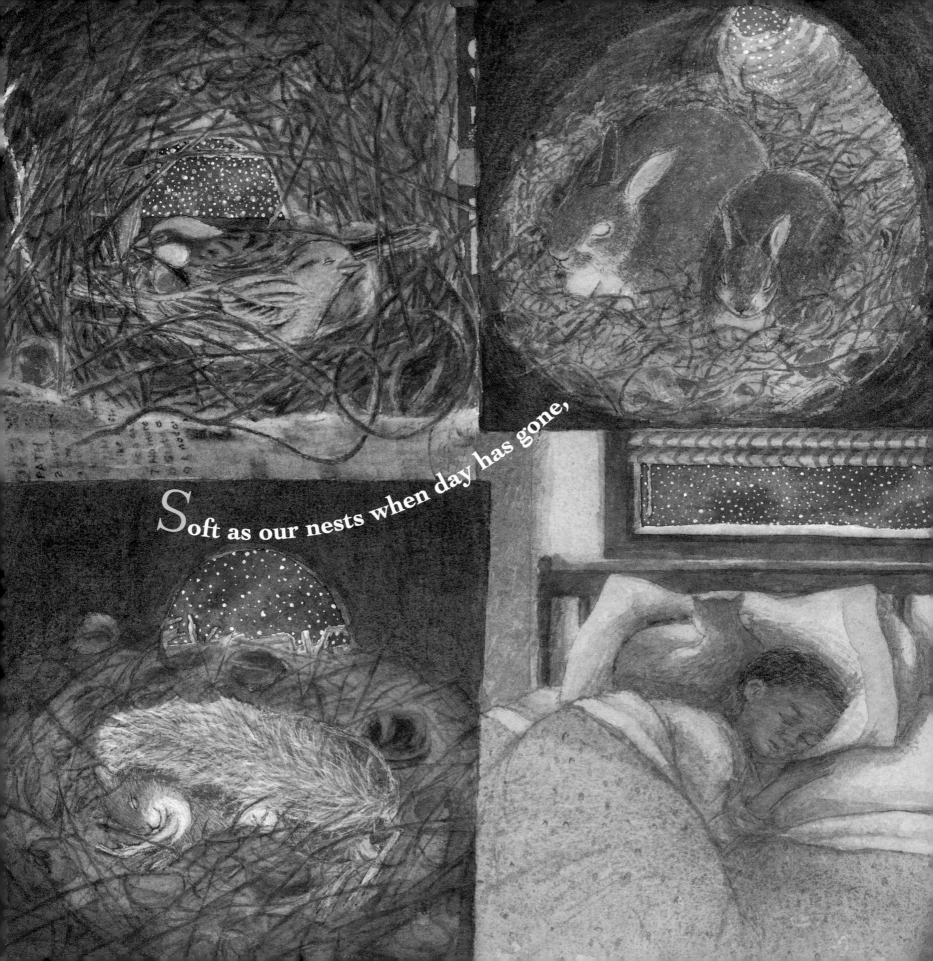

Soft as our nests when day has gone,

Snow came singing a silent song.

Night

was here,

but she

left at

dawn.

Shhhhhhhhh

Oops.

What is the sound of one bird hopping?

Does the deer

feel the cold   of the snow

in her hoofs?

hop hop hop hop hop

I think—

I think

I left it—

I think

I left it

here—

somewhere . . .

I think.

No, wait—

it here . . .

I left

I know

I think I—

No, did he get loose?

You say something like,
Hi.

I just opened the door to look out and he bolte

I say something like,
Hi.
Have you seen my dog?

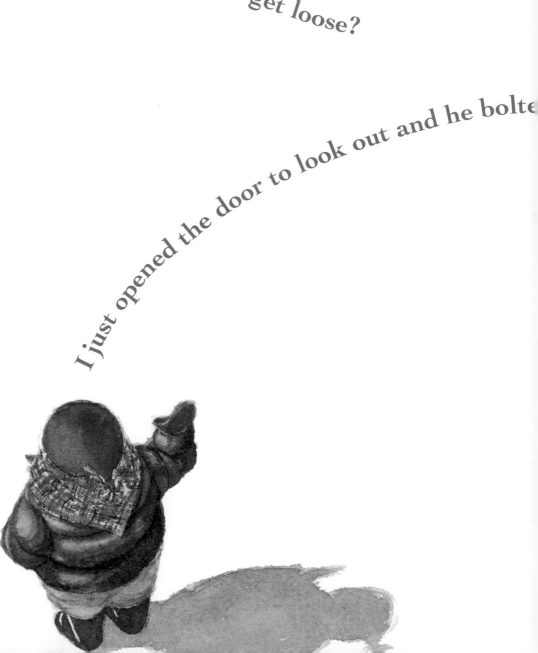

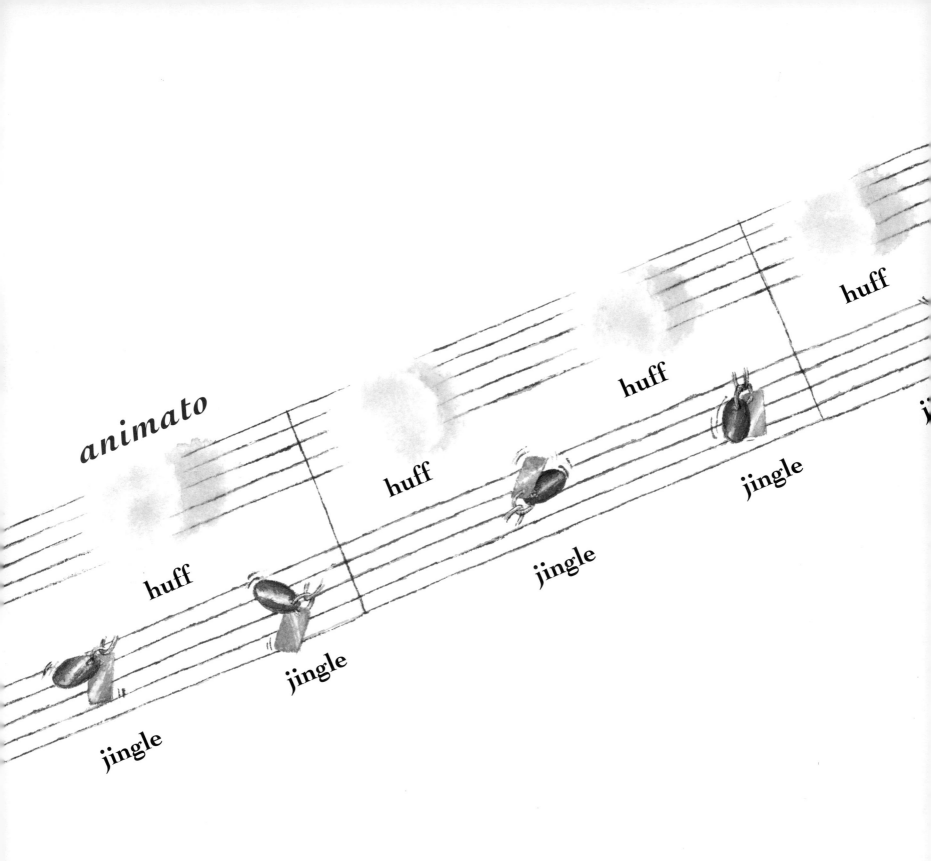

A CAR WENT BY

poot poot poot poot poot poot   poot poot poot poot . . .

Someone inside was drawing in the frost on the window.

plop

We could hear its radio playing. (Cover your mouth with your hand and sing a song from the radio.)

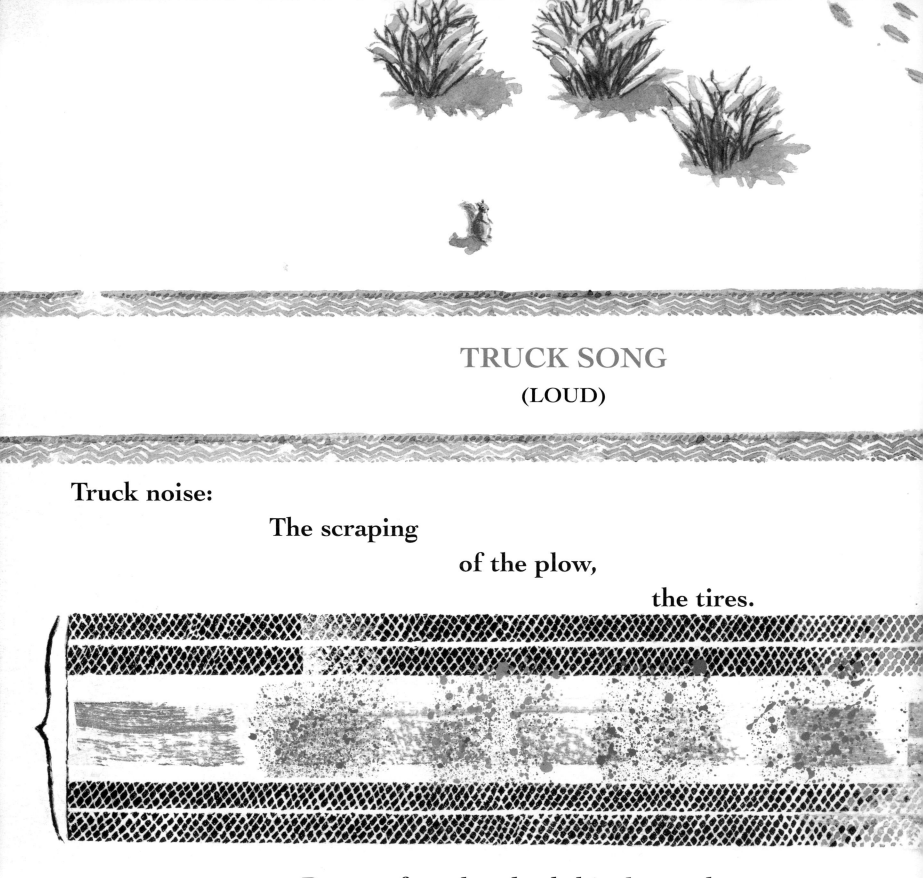

TRUCK SONG
(LOUD)

Truck noise:

The scraping

of the plow,

the tires.

Bursts of sand and salt hit the road.

Did you
find him?
No.
No.

All of us looking for something to eat.
The sun came looking for something to heat.

It found the snow, and the deer's cold feet.

There he is!
I see him!

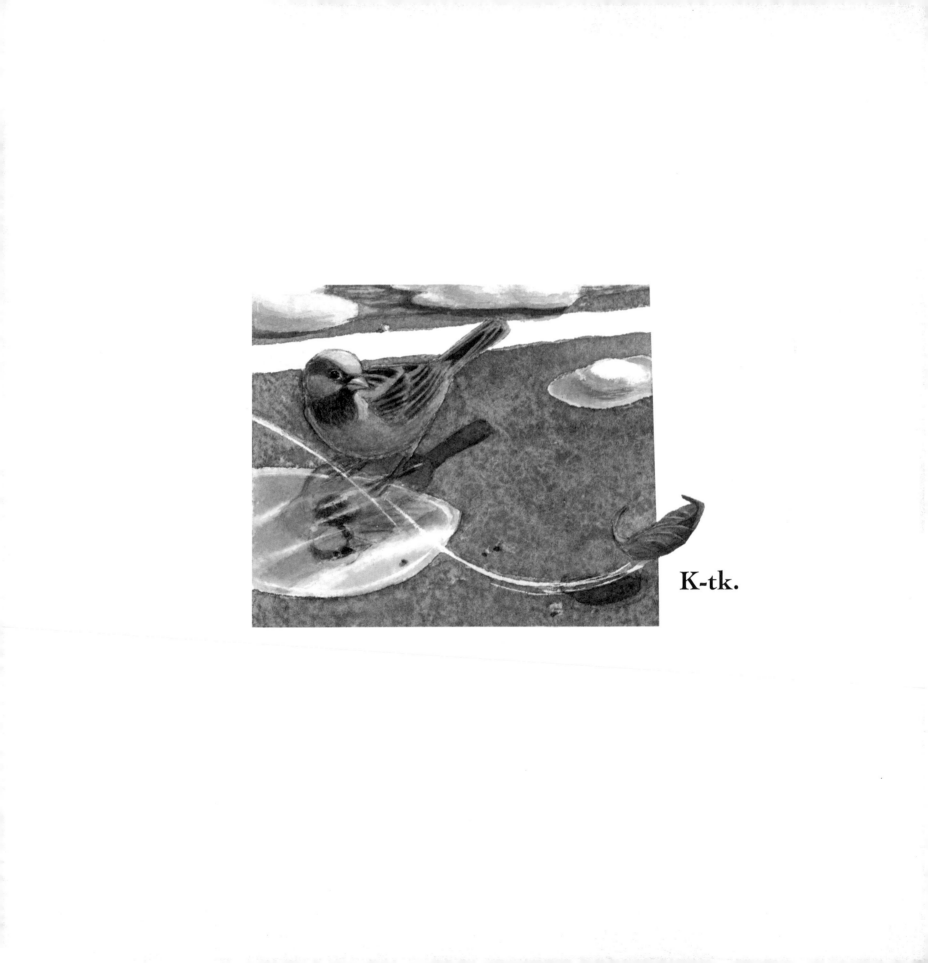

K-tk.

Good boy.

Why are you
saying he's good?

So he'll like
coming home.

Click.

Quick, and as quiet as a bunny on a road. Swift, and as silent as the shadow of a crow.

Clouds crept in and started to snow.

Everyone whisper:

For Bill and Lucky,
the great rogues

Snow Music

Copyright © 2003 by Lynne Rae Perkins

All rights reserved. Printed in the United States of America.

www.harperchildrens.com

Pen and ink and watercolor paints were used to prepare the full-color art.

The text type is 20-point Cochin Bold.

Library of Congress Cataloging-in-Publication Data

Perkins, Lynne Rae.

Snow music / by Lynne Rae Perkins.

p. cm.

"Greenwillow Books."

Summary: When a dog gets loose from the house on a snowy day, his owner searches
for him and experiences the sounds of various animals and things in the snow.

ISBN 0-06-623956-7 (trade). ISBN 0-06-623958-3 (lib. bdg.)

[1. Snow—Fiction. 2. Sound—Fiction. 3. Lost and found possessions—Fiction.

4. Dogs—Fiction.] I. Title.

PZ7.P4313 Sn 2003 [E]—dc21 2002192758

10 9 8 7 6 5 4 3

First Edition

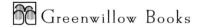 Greenwillow Books